Sleeping with the Light On

Sleeping with the Light On

David Unger

Illustrations by
Carlos Vélez Aguilera

GROUNDWOOD BOOKS
HOUSE OF ANANSI PRESS
TORONTO / BERKELEY

The text is based on the story "La Casita," first published in 2012
by CIDCLI Books, Mexico City, Mexico.

Groundwood Books / House of Anansi Press
groundwoodbooks.com

We gratefully acknowledge the Government of Canada for its financial
support of our publishing program.

With the participation of the Government of Canada
Avec la participation du gouvernement du Canada | Canadä

Library and Archives Canada Cataloguing in Publication
Title: Sleeping with the light on / David Unger ; illustrations by Carlos Vélez
Aguilera.
Names: Unger, David, author. | Vélez, Carlos, illustrator.
Identifiers: Canadiana (print) 20190225130 | Canadiana (ebook)
20190225203 | ISBN 9781773063843 (hardcover) | ISBN 9781773063850
(EPUB) | ISBN 9781773063867 (Kindle)
Classification: LCC PZ7.U64 Sle 2020 | DDC j813/.54—dc23

Jacket and interior illustrations by Carlos Vélez Aguilera
Jacket design by Michael Solomon

Groundwood Books is committed to protecting our natural environment. This
book is made of material from well-managed FSC®-certified forests, recycled
materials, and other controlled sources.

Printed and bound in Canada

MIX
Paper from
responsible sources
FSC C016245
FSC
www.fsc.org

To Luis and Fortuna,
who made La Casita our home

La Casita

My family lives on the second floor of La Casita — the Little House — in Guatemala City, Central America.

It's anything but little. That's because it's not just our home. It's also our restaurant.

There are eight wooden tables and lots and lots of fluffy chairs on the ground floor. A vase with fresh flowers sits on a big fancy table under a crystal chandelier right in the middle of the restaurant. The whole room seems to glow, especially at night when the lights are on. The wooden floors are polished like glass, and my parents make us tiptoe through the dining room so we won't smudge the floor. You can almost see your face in it.

La Casita has three windows that face the street. I like to sit on the windowsill and watch people walk by on the other side of the iron bars. Sometimes people smile. Sometimes they wave or even talk to me.

Once an Indian lady wearing a *huipil* and red ribbons in her black braids gave me two *canillas de leche* — chewy candies made of sugar and caramel. I gave one to my brother, Felipe.

My favorite room in La Casita used to be the kitchen. That was before I found out it was a dangerous place. It has two refrigerators. One is for chicken, fish and meat. The other one is for milk, fruits and vegetables.

The kitchen has huge metal sinks and lots of shiny pots and pans hanging on hooks above the sink. One wall has cabinets and cutting boards of all sizes on the counter. The other wall has a counter topped with large glass jars filled with rice and black beans.

And, of course, there's a gas stove. A pot of black beans always sits on the back burner next to a pot with boiled plantains. Yummy!

Everyone says La Casita is the best restaurant in Guatemala City. Since we never go out to eat, I don't really know. I do like our weekend brunch when we eat *tamales* and *chuchitos* that Consuelo, my nanny, prepares.

Once when Felipe and I were alone in the kitchen, he wanted to show off how much bigger he is. Whenever anyone asks our age, Felipe always says that he is two years older. But he is just twenty months older, which doesn't sound like a lot to me.

"I can do so many more things than you," he bragged. "My bicycle is bigger. And I know how to light the oven!"

"Like Augusto?"

"Faster than that, slowpoke!" He pulled over a kitchen stool, climbed up and snagged a box of matches from a shelf.

"Watch what I can do!" he said.

"Mamá says not to play with matches."

"Oh, man, don't be a baby." He turned the oven dial and lit a match.

The stove started to purr softly. I had the feeling that something bad was about to happen.

I stepped back.

Felipe said, "Don't be afraid!" Then he opened the oven door. "Now, where is it?" He stuck his head halfway into the oven.

"Where is what?"

"I can't find the hole where the gas comes out —"

KABOOM!

There was a huge explosion.

I screamed.

Felipe was thrown to the kitchen floor. He put his hands to his face and started to cry.

"I can't see! I can't see!"

Mamá rushed in from the dining room. She was holding the silverware.

"What happened?" she asked me. Her face was very crinkly.

By now I was crying, too. All I could do was point to the stove.

Mamá sniffed. The kitchen smelled of gas. She closed the oven door, turned the gas knob off and picked up Felipe, all in one motion.

I thought he had burned his face off!

But Felipe was all right. Mamá put ice in a towel on his face, and soon he stopped crying. Only a little bit of gas had slipped out.

But, boy, was he funny looking! It reminded me of the cartoon when Sylvester the Cat put Tweety Bird in the chimney and lit it. KABOOM!

Felipe's face was pink. He had burned off his eyebrows and eyelashes. Mamá put ointment on his face that made his skin smooth as a balloon. He kept complaining about how much it hurt.

I could have said something mean to him — called him a *bruto*, a birdbrain, for trying to light the stove. But I decided not to make him feel worse.

From then on, Felipe glared at the stove whenever he went into the kitchen, as if it were some kind of traitor.

The Magic Trick

In the kitchen, there is a big glass tank filled with lobsters. They are speckled creatures with long antennas and lots of warts on their legs. They all have funny names like Don Quixote, Superman, Hannibal, King Arthur and Genghis Khan.

One by one the lobsters disappear and are replaced.

All but Genghis Khan.

Genghis Khan is huge — about the size of a small dog. But since he lives underwater, he can't bark. Papá is so proud of his size. Sometimes he brings customers into the kitchen to see him. He says he will never let anyone eat him.

I can spend hours and hours watching the lobsters moving slowly along the bottom of the tank. Their shells must weigh a ton. They are as ugly as iguanas, except they live underwater.

When I press my face against the glass, I am sure they know I am here, yet they never react.

Only Genghis Khan comes up to my face. He stares at me through his small round eyes. He never blinks.

He is definitely the king. He climbs on the backs of the other lobsters and sticks his antennas all the way out of the water. It's as if he's using them to breathe. Maybe his antennas are like submarine periscopes.

What is he looking for? Maybe he is using them to try to find me.

If there were more lobsters in the tank, could Genghis Khan get out by climbing over them?

What if he can move faster on land than in the water? What if he chases after me like a dog?

Luckily, he can't get out. And there are rubber bands handcuffing his claws.

□

When Mamá takes Felipe to his piano classes after school, Consuelo, my *niñera*, looks after me.

One day she's very busy in the courtyard washing clothes in the *pila* and hanging them up on the laundry lines.

So I go into the kitchen and watch Augusto, the cook, preparing for dinner. He always wears a big stiff white apron and a puffy hat like the chef on the Cream of Wheat box. He rushes around slicing carrots, tomatoes and cucumbers so fast that the knife in his hand simply whizzes by.

When Augusto sees me, he puts a stool in front of the lobster tank for me. He knows I like staring through the glass to watch the lobsters move around.

A little while later, Otto, the waiter, runs in. He hurries into a little closet by the back door, takes off his street clothes and puts on a white shirt, black pants and a thin black tie.

Otto is skinny like a cane. He doesn't really like to talk to me, especially when he comes to work late.

Augusto calls me from the sink where he is washing vegetables.

"Davico, do you like magic?" he asks, drying his hands on his apron.

"I guess so. What's magic?"

"You know, tricks. Like when a magician puts a scarf in a hat and a moment later he pulls out a rabbit." He shows me the two gold teeth in his mouth.

"How can a scarf turn into a rabbit?"

Otto laughs, coming out of the closet. "Tell him that you are going to put him in a potato sack and we will see if he comes out a horse or a mule."

Augusto smiles and shakes his head at Otto, as if to tell him not to tease me.

He bends down in front of me and says, "Magicians do magic tricks. You know, like when your Uncle Aaron touches the back of your ear and pulls out a coin."

"That's magic?"

"That's magic! Would you like me to show you a trick?"

"Sure." I am so surprised Augusto is being nice to me. Usually he treats me like a pest.

"Come with me." Augusto grabs hold of my hand. He takes me to the lobster tank. When I glance at his face, I swear that he winks at Otto.

"Now I want you to turn around and stand here with your arms at your sides."

I turn around so my back is to the fish tank.

Otto, all smiles now, starts singing the Guatemalan national anthem. His thin mustache seems drawn by a pencil.

I begin to sing proudly along. I learned the song in school. I like the tune, but don't understand many of the words. Something confusing about a plow, a hangman, and not letting people spit on your face.

"Davico, now turn around and watch me," says Augusto.

He is standing between me and the tank.

His hands are behind his back, and water drips to the floor.

"Are you ready?"

"Sure," I say, standing straight as a soldier.

Augusto walks over to me. He's shorter than my father, but he wears lifts in his shoes to seem taller. His arms are thick like a fisherman's.

I stare at the red pimples on his face. Some of them have turned white. He rubs grease on his hair to make it shiny and stay in place.

He stops right in front of me. He is so close that his cologne tickles my nose. I begin to scratch it.

In one motion, Augusto whisks his hands behind my back. I think he is going to surprise me, give me a cookie or a *canilla de leche*.

My heart is really racing.

Suddenly I hear a clacking noise behind me.

Before I can turn around, Augusto spins a giant lobster in front of my face and yells, "Ta-dah! Davico, say hi to Genghis Khan."

He has taken the rubber bands off the lobster's claws and they are clacking in my face! I am afraid they will snap my nose or the antennas might poke out my eyes. My heart pounds in my chest like footsteps tromping up wooden stairs.

Augusto is smiling, as if he has done something courageous or clever.

"Look at his face!" he says, turning to Otto.

Otto's lips barely move as he lets out a squeaky laugh between his teeth. "The face of a bruto."

"I am not!" I scream at them.

They are so proud of themselves. My pants are wet and warm. I realize that Augusto's magic trick has made me make a little pipi. Tears stream down my face as I go up to my room to change.

I was wrong to think Augusto and Otto were my friends.

Papers Raining from the Sky

The week after Augusto plays his dirty trick on me, Consuelo takes me with her to buy tortillas at the corner store. I hear lots of airplanes flying low overhead.

Suddenly, yellow and blue papers rain down from the sky, twisting and spinning in the air. They land on the sidewalk and street like flying saucers.

On our way back, I pick up several sheets of paper to show my father.

He is reading the newspaper, sitting in one of the fluffy chairs in the dining room.

"What is it, Davico?"

"Airplanes dropped these pretty papers on the sidewalk."

Papá takes off his reading glasses and pronounces the words aloud very slowly. His face becomes angrier and angrier the more words he reads. He mutters words like *guns*, *armies* and *tanks*, which I know from my comics. But now the words make me shiver.

When he has finished reading, he rips the sheets of paper into dozens of pieces.

"What is it, Papá?"

"Trouble," he says. And he shakes his head.

I know the words on the paper have made him angry. I understand some of them, but many, like *liberación* and *revolución*, I really don't.

"What kind of trouble?"

"These flyers are warning us of trouble to come. Dirty politics."

"What's dirty politics?"

My father runs a hand through his hair. It is beginning to thin and turn silvery.

"Davico, I came to Guatemala from Germany to escape this nonsense."

"What nonsense?"

He smiles at me. "It's too complicated to explain to you."

"No, it's not! I am learning to add and subtract numbers in school. I can read some chapter books. Señorita Elisa says I am very smart."

My father stands up and hugs me. He hardly ever touches me. Maybe these colored papers aren't so bad.

While he is hugging me, I tell him, "Felipe also tells me lots of interesting things. The other day he told me that the Mayans built giant temples in the jungle."

My father stops hugging me and looks away, scratching at his knuckles. "It's nothing for you to worry about."

He pulls me by the hand and we go out into the courtyard. He looks up into the air. More papers are flying down. His face darkens.

Suddenly he shouts, "Why can't people leave us alone?" And he goes off by himself into the house.

I stay in the courtyard and pick up the papers. Maybe Felipe can explain the big words to me later.

For now, I try to figure out what is bothering Papá. A few days ago, we heard loud sirens going off and then some shooting. Mamá said it was probably just some older kids throwing firecrackers. But I know what firecrackers sound like.

And these were not the sounds of fire-crackers.

□

The restaurant is almost always empty at night now. I am sure it has to do with the colored papers that came flying down. All I can think is that people are afraid to go out.

One night the electricity goes out after the last customers leave. Mamá lights some big stumpy candles. Papá locks the big wooden door and puts the metal latch across the front.

Sirens are screaming. Maybe a fire truck is racing to a fire, or a police car is hurrying to an accident.

But then we hear people running down the street, and the sound of guns and rifles going off.

I am very scared. Even Felipe looks frightened. Our parents hug us as we eat warm tortillas, black beans and cheese under the dining-room table.

There is nothing more we can do. We huddle together and listen to the government radio station for news.

The sirens? I know they hurt my ears and don't come from police cars or ambulances.

This goes on for several nights in a row.

"What are we going to do?" asks Mamá on the third night as we sit under the largest dining-room table. "The president says that these blackouts are necessary because soldiers are planning to invade Guatemala City and take control."

Papá shrugs. He has got real good at shrugging. "That's what the flyers said."

"The flyers I found on the street?" I ask.

In the candlelight, my father's face looks like a ghost.

"Yes," he sighs.

Felipe pipes in. "The president is turning off the electricity so that the invaders won't bomb his palace. I would do the same thing."

"Is Felipe right?" I ask.

My mother taps my leg to tell me to quiet down. Then she says, "We have to do something, Luis. We can't just sit here and wait. Soon we will have to close up the restaurant for good."

Papá shrugs. "Well, at least people can still come for lunch."

"Just our friends who work in the hotels and stores nearby. And the newspaper reporters from the United States. They never order more than a sandwich and a beer," my mother says, rolling her eyes. "If these blackouts continue, we'll have to throw out the beef and chicken in the freezer."

"I know that," Papá says sharply.

"Luis, please. Don't raise your voice at me —"

For a second, there is silence. I hate it when my parents fight. I look at Felipe. He just turns away.

"Are you going to have to close the restaurant?" I ask.

Felipe snaps back at me. "The restaurant is finished."

I wonder if Consuelo is safe. I worry about the lobsters. They would all die if a bullet were to fly in and hit the glass tank.

"Yes, yes. I'm sorry, Fortuna. We have to do something," Papá says. He hugs my mamá. She runs her hand through his hair, and my father smiles his tiny crooked smile.

This makes me happy.

I have the feeling that everything will be okay.

The Park

On Saturday, Consuelo takes Felipe and me to the park in front of the National Palace. I ride my green bike and my brother his red bike. Consuelo sits on a bench and talks to an Indian lady. They could be sisters, they look so much alike, except Consuelo wears a white blouse, a black skirt and black shoes. The Indian lady has a huipil and a *corte*, and she is barefoot.

All the time she is talking, Consuelo doesn't take her eye off us zipping around the fountain. There are pigeons flying everywhere. When Felipe and I get tired, we sit on a bench on the other side of the fountain, but where Consuelo can still see us.

The National Palace is made of green stone. It looks like a big avocado. The front is lined with dozens of soldiers sitting on the steps. Rifles hang across their chests. They are talking to one another.

I look up at the many palace windows. I wonder which is the president's window. Does he hear the sirens wailing at night?

I am afraid to ask Felipe questions because he always seems so angry now.

"Is this where the president lives?"

"Lives or works. What's the difference? An airplane could drop a bomb from the sky, and then poof! He'd be a goner!"

I should be scared, but I am not. Everything seems so unreal. It's as if the green palace and the soldiers are in a movie. Even the clouds look fake.

A shoeshine boy comes up to us.

"Shoeshine?" he asks in English. "Cheap."

"No queremos, gracias," Felipe answers in Spanish, shaking his head.

The boy is barefoot. His clothes are dirty. His hair is matted down and he has streaks of black shoe polish on his brown face. He might be twice my age. He is so thin and bony. I wonder where he lives. Probably on the streets.

"Ten cents," he says.

"No, gracias."

"Cinco centavos," he finally says. He's desperate.

When it is clear that we don't want a shoeshine, he points to the palace. "The gringos are coming."

"What are gringos?" I ask.

"People from the United States of America!" Felipe snaps. And then he turns to the shoeshine boy. "How do you know?"

The shoeshine boy lifts his left arm. It is splotched with brown and black polish. His left hand is missing the little finger! I want to ask him how he lost it.

"Don't you see all the tanks?"

Felipe and I stand up on the bench. Sure enough, in the distance, there are three dark green tanks. They look like gigantic turtles. Each one has a long green gun that looks like a telescope. Soldiers dressed in brown uniforms are sitting on top of them.

"The gringos are coming, the gringos are coming!" the shoeshine boy chants, standing up, pointing. "That's what everyone says!"

Two men in suits are walking briskly across the park, scaring up the pigeons. Hundreds of birds are flying overhead. The sun has darted behind a big fat cloud. It suddenly turns cold.

"The gringos are coming, the gringos are coming!" the shoeshine boy shouts, pointing to the two men who go up the National Palace steps.

I don't think this boy goes to school. Where does he find these things out? He seems to know things even my parents don't know.

"Shut up, *ishto*!" I blurt out, saying a Mayan word I shouldn't say. It isn't such a horrible word, like calling him a brat. I say it to make the boy feel bad and for me to feel better.

He puts down his shoeshine case. "Take it back, or I'll smack you —"

Felipe and I look at each other. We are both scared. We quickly get on our bikes and ride back to Consuelo. Out of breath, we beg her to take us home immediately.

Consuelo stands up in a huff, not happy to go back home.

"You two look like you have seen the devil."

"Just take us home. Please."

"It wasn't smart to call that shoeshine boy an ishto. He could have beat us up," Felipe says on our way back. "Still, it was brave of you."

I feel a bit better on the ride home. Maybe I'm not such a scaredy cat!

Then I remember the soldiers and the tanks. My body shivers.

The Night Lamp

One evening after dinner, Felipe and I go up-
stairs to play pick-up sticks in our bedroom.
The electricity is still on. Maybe things are
back to normal.

Suddenly we hear loud *pow-pows*.

I would like to think it is a car backfiring,
but I recognize the sound of gunfire now. I
don't know who is shooting at whom and

I don't care. I just want my parents to stop worrying. For things to get back to normal.

The lights go out. Footsteps pound on the staircase.

Mamá appears at the door. She is out of breath.

"Grab your pillow and blanket, Davico. You, too, Felipe. *Hurry!*"

"Why?" Felipe wails. He is very close to winning the game.

"I want both of you downstairs."

"That's no explanation!" he snaps back.

"It's enough that I say so!"

Felipe grabs his brown dirty dog Chucho by an ear and trudges to the staircase. He couldn't walk any slower.

I carry Gordito, the pink pig that spends every night on my pillow.

Gordito and Chucho are useless. They can't stop the blackouts. Or the shooting.

Our parents shout orders to each other.

They are running around grabbing blankets and pillows. Their faces are full of sweat.

The gunfire sounds louder than ever.

They use the blankets to make beds for us underneath the big table in the middle of the restaurant. They put the chairs around us like guards.

But I am happy to have the whole family sleeping together, wrapped in blankets. There's barely enough room for all of us. I only have to stretch my arms to touch a warm body.

I could get used to sleeping like this. Bullets and blackouts make my life more interesting. I would rather sleep under the table than sleep alone in bed with Gordito.

The shooting stops and the electricity comes back on. We are still wide awake. Mamá sends us back to our room. We have to sleep with the lights out.

When the blackouts began, my father bought me a battery lamp so I could sleep with a light on. The lamp has a revolving shade. When it turns, sun, clouds and waves roll across the light. I imagine waves crashing on a beach, sending up sprays of water.

"Are you going to sleep with that stupid lamp on again?" Felipe asks.

"Why do you care?"

"The lamp keeps me awake."

"But I need it to fall asleep."

"Because of the shooting? You're just a big baby."

I like the lamp, even when Consuelo leaves a shirt hanging on my closet doorknob. When the wind blows through the open window, I see shadows dancing on the white walls. I can't control my mind. If the wind blows, my shirt billows out like a huge monster trying to snatch at me. Then the scratches on the walls are spiders or snakes. If I hear whistling in the streets, I'm sure that it's a bat trying to fly into our bedroom.

But I can only fall sleep with the battery light after hearing the shooting.

Later that night I feel tears coming out of my eyes.

"Felipe, are you okay?"

"Of course I'm okay." I can hear him also whimpering.

"Do you want to come into my bed?"

He waits a minute before answering. "If you pee in bed, I will never speak to you again," he says, stirring.

Felipe and Chucho come into my bed. We fall asleep back to back, both of us hugging our stuffed animals.

Blackouts

The blackouts happen every night. The telephone in the restaurant hardly ever rings. Otto and Augusto stop working for us. La Casita opens only for lunch. Mamá cooks and Papá is the waiter.

Felipe and I cannot go to school. Guatemala City is too dangerous. We are on an endless vacation.

"Davico, no more sitting on the window-sill!" Papá says.

"But why?"

"We must keep the shutters closed, even when we open the restaurant for lunch. We want things to be safe."

"Why?"

Papá digs into his pocket and pulls out a flat piece of metal. "Look what I found in a wall when I went shopping this morning."

Felipe has been reading a comic in one of the restaurant chairs. He comes over.

"Is it an old coin?" he asks.

"No," Papá breathes out. "It is a bullet."

"Is it from the tanks?" I ask.

"No, it's from a gun."

"Was someone shooting at you?" Felipe asks, examining the bullet.

"Oh, no," he says. "It was stuck in a wall waiting for me to take it."

"Are we at war?" I ask.

"We aren't at war yet. But the buildings are full of bullet holes. Thank goodness for the American reporters. Otherwise, we would have to close."

"Are the reporters the gringos?" I ask.

My father looks at me funny. "Where did you learn that word?"

"From the shoeshine boy."

"A shoeshine boy," my father repeats. "Maybe he knows more of what is going on in this country than the president. Who is going to protect us?"

I don't want my father to ask questions. He should know the answers.

□

Consuelo doesn't take us to feed bananas to La Mocosita, the baby elephant at the zoo. We don't go to watch the crocodiles sunning at the edge of a pool.

Felipe and I play with my electric train so much that we crash it against a wall. We twist the rails and take apart the cars by pulling off the doors and windows.

Who cares?

□

Consuelo stops taking us to the park to ride our bicycles around the fountain in front of the National Palace. I miss the ficus trees, the blackbirds, the sprays of water, the shoeshine boys.

I even miss the dirty pigeons.

"Why can't we go?" we ask.

"Soldiers are camped out in tents under the trees," my father says. "They are expecting an invasion any day."

I don't know what an invasion is, but it can't be good since Papá frowns when he says the word. I imagine it might mean there will be other enemy soldiers coming to the palace to fight with the president's men. I think about the animals in the zoo and realize we are stuck in a cage, too. But the animals have it better than us. They can move around in the sun.

One night we are all sleeping under the big dining-room table. I hear airplanes flying overhead. Then the sirens start to wail again. Felipe is asleep next to me. I hear lots of gunfire. Maybe the invasion is beginning.

"Guatemala is too dangerous," Papá says. "What if a bomb —"

"Don't say it!" Mamá says harshly. "The children are right here."

"We need to get out of here soon, Fortuna."

I close my eyes to pretend I'm sleeping. It's so dark they can't see me anyway.

"People are afraid to go out. The rebel radio station says thousands of soldiers are just outside the city, waiting for orders. The government is going to be overthrown," says Papá.

I don't understand who is throwing things over, but it can't be good. I am sure my father is frowning.

"Maybe we can ask the American reporters for help getting out," my mother says.

I hear the blankets moving around. I hope my parents are hugging each other the way I like.

"I didn't leave Germany to die like a dog in Guatemala."

"We have to be careful of what we say," Mamá hushes. "The neighbors may hear us —"

"We can't trust anyone. Otto was serious when he said to me that one day the restaurant will be his."

"Even the walls have ears," Mamá says.

"Like they had in Germany."

Walls with ears. I imagine all these big hairy ears stuck to the wall and perking up whenever they hear a sound.

I am very confused. The American reporters are also gringos. Are they good? They must be. Are Mamá and Papá thinking of going to gringo-land?

I close my eyes and clutch Gordito. This is a good moment to fall asleep.

Going to Jail

The next day at breakfast, Mamá tells us that she and Papá have decided to go to a place called the United States of America.

"What's that?"

"You mean *Where's* that!" Felipe yells, pushing a finger into my ribs.

Why is he so angry at me now? Has he forgotten that we slept together when both of us were scared, and I didn't pee in bed?

My mother touches my hair. "Far away. They speak English there."

"You mean I won't be able to speak Spanish anymore?"

Before our parents can answer, Felipe says, "English is a strange language. I am studying it in school."

"You *were* studying it in school," I correct my brother, the way he corrects me. "Your prepa is closed."

Felipe kicks my chair hard.

"Stop that, right now!" my mother scolds.

He glares at Mamá. "English is so stupid! It's a language for gringos!"

"I speak English. So does Papá. It's a good language. You will both learn it so fast!"

"They say 'table' for *mesa* and 'book' for *libro*," says Felipe.

My mother smiles her tired smile. "It's another way of saying things, that's all."

Felipe shakes his head. He looks miserable.

"What about La Casita? Will we take the restaurant with us?" I don't even feel like finishing my *pan francés* and cheese. The thought of living in another house makes me sick.

Felipe just shakes his head again, groaning. He looks at me as if I am the enemy and he would be happy to kill me. "You are as stupid as English. You know that?"

Mamá hushes him.

"No," she says. "La Casita stays here. This is not our building. We rent it. Maybe someone will buy the business. Your father and I will go first to the United States to look for new jobs and a new house."

"But what about us? Will we have to sleep alone on the benches in the park like the shoeshine boy?"

"You will stay with your Uncle Aaron," my mother says.

"Uncle Aaron?" Felipe says in disbelief. He throws the sweet roll he was eating across the table. He stamps his feet. "I'm not going! I'd rather live on the streets!"

Uncle Aaron is very tall and bald. He has batwing glasses and always wears a gray suit with a vest. I don't think I have ever heard him laugh.

He does know how to do a coin trick behind my ear. But he does it without smiling, as if magic were like taking a bath or eating carrots.

This whole time Papá is drinking coffee and reading the newspaper. Every once in a while he shakes his head.

"Aunt Lonia always shouts at us. Don't do this, don't do that." Felipe continues in a moping voice.

"She will be different this time. You'll see."

Aunt Lonia is very pretty, but she is always yelling. Keep your feet off this. Don't put your hands in that! Why are you two always fighting?

She is a grump.

Felipe is right. Who in the world would want to stay with them?

"Why can't we go with you?" Felipe asks.

I nod. "We won't be any trouble. We won't fight or argue."

"We have to look for jobs," Mamá says.

"I can look for a job," I say.

Felipe and Mamá laugh. Did I say something funny?

"Why doesn't Davico think before he speaks?"

I don't understand what is going on. Felipe is sometimes a good friend. But the next moment, he makes fun of me.

"Can Consuelo come with us?" I ask.

"There's no room for her at Uncle Aaron's. Besides, they have their own maid, Tina. Maybe later, she'll join us in the United States."

"Consuelo is not a maid. She's our nanny. She won't like it if we go without her."

"We can recommend her for another job," Papá pipes in.

There are tears in my eyes.

"What about Genghis Khan? You said you would never get rid of him."

Felipe pushes his chair away from the table. He glares at me. "Why do you care so much about that big ugly lobster?" Then he marches up to our room.

"You haven't finished your breakfast," Mamá calls.

"I am not hungry," he says, already climbing the stairs.

"You haven't been told you can get up from the table."

"I'm not hungry, either," I cry, following Felipe.

One thing is for sure. I have never been there, but I already hate the United States.

One day, before we have to leave La Casita, I go downstairs to say goodbye to the lobsters. The kitchen is totally empty. Gone are the pots, the pans and the cutting boards. The lobster tank has been drained and placed in a corner by the back door.

All the lobsters are gone, including Genghis Khan.

I should ask what happened to him, but I don't.

Maybe someone bought him and ate him.

I don't want to know.

Jail

A week later, our parents take us to Uncle Aaron's house in a taxi. They give us lots of wet kisses at the door. I am crying. So is Felipe.

"We will send for you soon. As soon as we find jobs."

"Where are you going?"

"To Chicago. We have some friends there. They have children, too."

And then they drive off to the airport with their suitcases.

Uncle Aaron and Aunt Lonia live in a huge wooden house with a large yard. They have two boxers, Farouk and Mosqueta, who are always barking. My aunt and uncle live in a part of Guatemala City that only has houses. It is so far from La Casita, it might as well be on the moon.

Maybe I will never see the National Palace or the fountain in the park again. Or pigeons. Or shoeshine boys.

Every morning, my aunt and uncle go off to work in separate cars. Uncle Aaron goes to his office for the whole day. Aunt Lonia works only in the morning at a store that sells bras and underpants.

Tina, the maid, keeps watch over us. She is not like Consuelo. She's like a soldier or a jailer who lets Aunt Lonia know whenever we do something wrong.

The first few days we're only allowed to play card games and read comic books. Aunt Lonia suggests that Felipe write to our parents and tell them how we are doing.

What will Felipe write to them about? How bored we are?

Then Tina says we can go into the front yard, but we're afraid that the dogs will jump all over us and maybe bite us. They have huge teeth and big fat lips, which swim in white foam when they growl.

Aunt Lonia comes home for lunch. She won't let us ride our bikes in the house.

"You'll break a lamp or one of my vases."

"We promise not to."

"No. No. And you will leave tire marks on the wooden floor."

She has answers for everything.

Our bicycles have to stay outside. We can't even touch them because the back door is always latched.

Nothing's the same. I miss the shiny pots and the lobster tank.

From the kitchen window I notice that our bikes have become homes for spiders.

One day I see a huge rat gnawing on the wheel of my two-wheeler.

"Aunt Lonia! I saw a rat trying to eat my bicycle."

"Nonsense. Your bike is made of steel."

"It was biting the tires."

"Tires are made of rubber." She laughs as if I've said something ridiculous.

I want to cry. Cry as loud as I can. But I feel that my heart is stopped up.

Felipe says that Aunt Lonia doesn't care about us.

"Even the rats are having more fun than us," he says sadly.

□

It is the rainy season in Guatemala. Every morning Felipe and I play checkers, pick-up sticks and cards to pass the time. Sometimes we are allowed to watch cartoons of Donald Duck, Mickey Mouse and Bugs Bunny on the TV.

We never go out.

Every afternoon, as soon as we finish lunch and Uncle Aaron goes back to work, Felipe and I put on our record of Cri-Cri songs. Felipe's favorite is "El Burrito," but I really like "El Chorrito."

It's a song about a fountain that's feeling hot, so it is in a very bad mood. Then an ant walks by with her umbrella and gets splashed by the fountain. She also gets into a bad mood because the water makes her pretty makeup run down her little cheeks.

I like the song because even though the music is happy, everyone is in a bad mood.

Just like us.

Sometimes I wonder what life will be like in the United States. Will it be hot or cold? Does it have mountains and volcanoes? Will anyone speak Spanish to me?

Cartoons don't really show what life would be like there.

Meanwhile, every day is the same. It is always rainy and sometimes it is cold. We play games. We listen to music. We are bored.

One day when the boxers are chained in the front yard, we manage to open the back door and look at our bicycles. The tires are flat. Spiderwebs are growing on the spokes. The paint has begun to peel.

We both curl up our fists in anger, but there is nothing we can do. The rain shoos us back indoors.

We are in a jail. We can walk around, but we can't escape. We watch tons and tons of television, lots of Bugs Bunny and Elmer

Fudd cartoons. But we don't find them funny anymore.

I miss my parents. I miss Consuelo and Otto. Scary Genghis Khan. Even mean old Augusto.

Every time I ask Uncle Aaron about my parents, he says that he doesn't know what they are doing. I ask him to call them, but he says no, it is too expensive.

I wonder if they are feeling lonely, too. Maybe they've forgotten about us while they look for jobs and a new place to live.

Maybe they have adopted new children.

9

Leaving Guatemala

One day when I am about to explode in tears, Aunt Lonia says, "You're going to join your parents!"

"In Chicago?" I ask.

In all the weeks Mamá and Papá have been away, we only got one letter from them. They complained about the cold and the snow and how hard it was to get jobs.

"You're going to Miami, Florida."

"What happened to Chicago?" Felipe whines. He has memorized all the players on both the Chicago White Sox and the Chicago Cubs. "What about Lake Michigan and Wrigley Field?"

"Maybe Miami, Florida, has a baseball team," I say, touching his arm.

He pulls away from me as if I were poison. "It doesn't, bruto."

Aunt Lonia locks him up in another room for calling me stupid. When she comes back, I ask her where Miami, Florida, is.

"It's very far away. You'll have to take an airplane to get there."

"We will fly through the air. Then we will be with my parents."

"That's right. You'll be able to go around by yourself," my aunt says. "Not like here." At least she recognizes that we have been treated like prisoners.

Still, I am sure that I will hate Miami, Florida, in the United States of America, for taking me away from so many of the things I love.

□

Felipe and I wear matching suits, shirts, ties and shoes to go on the airplane. Everyone thinks we're *cuaches* — twins — though I'm a bit smaller.

Felipe and I sit next to each other. A woman in a blue uniform gives us coloring books. We are also served a meal with chicken, rice and peas. They give us cloth napkins and silverware.

It feels as if we are in a restaurant, but the food isn't good like at home.

The airplane flies in the sky and goes straight through clouds, slicing them without getting hurt. Everything below us seems so far away. We see buildings, mountains, then oceans and islands. But no people. I know they must be down there, but I can't see them.

It all feels very strange, going to a place we've never seen before.

After we land, the woman in the blue uniform gives a special pin to Felipe. "You're the sky king," she says in English.

She gives me the same pin, but says, "You're the sky captain."

I smile though I don't know what the words mean.

□

The woman in the blue uniform opens the airplane door. As soon as we reach the top of the staircase to get off the plane, very hot gusts of wind slam our faces.

I look down from the airplane and see Mamá and Papá down below the metal staircase. They are very small. The asphalt shimmers because it is so hot.

Felipe and I run down the steps, crying.

I didn't know I had missed my parents so much. My mother looks the same. My father looks older and more wrinkly.

They are dressed funny. Papá is wearing a short-sleeve shirt and shorts instead of his usual suit. My mother is wearing shorts.

For the first time, I am seeing their legs!

Miami, Florida, is a strange place.

We walk over to a car. Mamá has learned to drive. So has Papá, but driving makes him too nervous.

As Mamá drives us home, I notice that Miami is flat as a pancake. No mountains or volcanoes like in Guatemala. Just buildings and trees. And lots of cars. Nobody seems to be walking.

Even though all the car windows are open, it's very hot. I'm sweating. Everything is sweating. Even our seat.

I realize that I will never wear the pants and sweaters I brought from Guatemala.

My mother stops the car. There's a big tree in front of a small house. A tall pine tree arches over the white tiled roof.

We get out of the car and see people coming over to us. They are also all wearing shorts.

They shake our hands, telling us that they are Mr. and Mrs. Denny and Mr. and Mrs. Beaver. Mamá tells us in Spanish that they are our new neighbors.

10

Forgetting Spanish

□

The clouds are different in Miami. Not as puffy. The sky seems so big and wide. It makes me feel very small.

In Guatemala, we had a courtyard with plants and small bushes. In Florida we have a lemon, mango and kumquat tree in a big backyard.

We borrow bicycles to reach the corner store. We find boxes of candies called Three

Musketeers, Mars and Snickers. And lots of bottles of Coca-Cola.

There are no *roscas*, *espumillas* and *canillas de leche*.

My parents can't buy black beans, yucca or plantains.

The avocados are big and watery.

No one speaks Spanish.

My mother hardly speaks Spanish to us anymore.

She says we will make lots of new friends.

So what if there aren't mountains and volcanoes?

I promise Mamá and Papá lots of things:

Not to speak Spanish at school.

Not to complain about the food.

To learn English.

Before long, this is all I remember of Spanish.

Buenos días.

Tengo hambre.

Necesito hacer pipí.

Forgetting Spanish. This is what coming to the United States means to me.

□

But there are some good things.

We can go outside into our backyard whenever we want. We don't need Consuelo to take us places.

The Miami newspaper interviews Papá. He tells the reporter that he is happy to be out of Guatemala. Away from the shooting and blackouts.

When the article comes out, there's a picture of all of us sitting and smiling together on our sofa. The writer refers to Papá and Mamá as a German couple because he was born in Germany. That makes him very angry. He's upset, also, that the man makes up a story that says Papá is happy to be in a free country, the United States of America, and that he can't wait to pay taxes.

He says he never said this.

Little by little I am beginning to like hot dogs, french fries and hamburgers, especially if we go out to dinner at Mae and Dave's. Still, it is strange to see people sitting on stools all in a row eating hot dogs and hamburgers and drinking bottle after bottle of something called root beer.

Not talking to one another.

□

One day we get into the car and drive for forty-five minutes until we get to a beach. For the first time in my life I see coconut trees, white sand and blue waves.

I really like running into the warm water, being able to jump in, and then feeling the sun tingling on my skin.

I don't know how, but I learn to swim on my very first day.

I am learning English in school and I like it. My teacher, Mrs. Rose, has huge freckles on her face and is always smiling. She puts her arms around all the students and makes us feel special.

I especially like her when she wears a red dress and sandals. She looks so pretty. I try to count all the freckles on her legs.

I learn to play baseball. I am bad at fielding, but I have learned to hit. Soon I will be able to bunt.

I am suddenly feeling very happy.

Joe Alvarez is our only neighbor who speaks Spanish. He has three daughters named Cookie, Nancy and Francine. And then there's Little Joe, but he is still a baby.

Mr. Alvarez takes us with Cookie and Nancy to Miami Stadium where we see the Miami Marlins beat the Tampa Tarpons.

He buys Felipe and me each a hot dog and a Coca-Cola. He gets the Miami players to autograph our baseballs!

My father says he misses Guatemala where he had work. He is having a hard time getting a job, though my mom is hired as a salesgirl at Burdines.

Papá says that when he gets a job, he'll buy Felipe and me new three-speed bicycles made by an American company named Schwinn.

He is so different from the American fathers. Papá is older, more serious. He has an accent when he speaks. He doesn't fit in like he did in Guatemala.

□

I am fitting in, learning to put ketchup on everything.

But on certain nights, I miss my lamp with the painted sun. Even my shirt on the doorknob.

I miss sleeping under the table when the lights go out.

I miss the blue and yellow papers twirling in the sky and falling into the courtyard.

I really miss Consuelo and how she would hold my hand when she took me places.

I miss mean Augusto and skinny old Otto.

I miss the lobsters in the kitchen, with their warts and their hairy legs.

Especially Genghis Khan.

Author's Note

In 1954, the year before our family left Guatemala, the United States paid a small group of soldiers to invade Guatemala. By dropping leaflets from airplanes and by scaring Guatemalans in radio broadcasts, the Americans forced our president to leave office. This was the start of a forty-year civil war in which 200,000 people died and half a million Guatemalans left the country.

Guatemalans are still leaving their homeland, trying to find a country where they can live in peace.

DAVID UNGER is an award-winning translator and author born in Guatemala. In 2014 he was awarded Guatemala's highest literary prize, the Miguel Ángel Asturias National Prize in Literature. He is the US representative for the Guadalajara Book Fair and teaches at City College in New York City.

CARLOS VÉLEZ AGUILERA is an editorial illustrator and comics artist who has illustrated more than twenty children's books, and he is the author-illustrator of the graphic novel *Salón Destino*. Carlos lives in Mexico City.